GETTING WHAT I DESERVE

RICH SAMUELS

RICH PERCEPTIONS

Getting What I Deserve

Rich Samuels

Rich Perceptions

This book is a work of fiction. Names, characters, places, and incidents are the product of the author's imagination or are used fictitiously. Any resemblance to actual events, locales, or persons, living or dead, is entirely coincidental.

No portion of this book may be reproduced in any form without written permission from the publisher or author, except as permitted by U.S. copyright law.

Copyright © 2024 by Rich Samuels

All rights reserved

Cover Design by Sam Rapp

ISBN 979-8-9873292-8-3

Contact: Rich@RichPerceptions.com

This is an independently published novel. Please consider leaving a review on your favorite site or at https://RichPercpetions.com

Content Advisory

This book honestly explores themes of toxic friendships and bullying and their potential impact on an individual's well-being. It contains references to verbal, emotional, and physical bullying experiences, feelings of anxiety, fear, insecurity, and loss of self-confidence.

While the story depicts the challenges faced by the protagonist, *it also portrays his resilience and emergence as a stronger person.*

Contents

Chapter 1	XI
1. Choice	1
2. How it Began	3
3. The Visit	13
4. Control	17
5. You Really Need to Grow Up	23
6. Things Get Complicated	31
7. Anxiety	35
8. The Shower	39
9. The Sleepover	45
10. Lucky Me	51
11. The Experiment	57
12. A Good Friend	65
13. I'm in Charge	69

14.	Liar	75
15.	The Hike	81
16.	This Is What You Did To Your Friend	85
17.	The Best Hamburger	91
18.	Did You Tell Them?	99
19.	Charlie Day	105
20.	Rage	109
21.	Getting What I Deserve	115

Resources	123
A Note from the Author	125
Also by Rich Samuels	127

Getting What I Deserve

1

Choice

I can't explain exactly how I felt.

Was it fear? Sure.

Anger? Definitely.

Frustration? Infinitely.

Confusion? One hundred percent.

But I opened the door anyway.

And I'm still trying to figure out if I made the right choice.

2

How it Began

Mark and I had known each other since we were nine years old. We weren't best friends, but we weren't enemies either. We'd say *hi* if we saw each other at lunch, or sometimes we'd end up side by side in class, but nothing more.

For the longest time, Mark was just a school friend that I would never see after school. He had his interests, which were a mystery to me, and I had mine, which were a mystery to him. We both laughed at the same jokes sometimes, but that was about the extent of our relationship.

As soon as we started middle school, Mark changed. For whatever reason, he started focusing on me in the wrong way. He rolled his eyes every time I talked and laughed pointlessly at my clothes (regardless of what I wore), my height (it wasn't like I chose to be shorter than him), and even how I walked (seriously?). I felt nothing but constant contempt from day one.

Mark and I ended up in the same English class. Even worse, Mr. Blake had assigned seating, and on the first day, I discovered we had to share a desk. He didn't waste any time. He raised his hand and asked loudly, "Can I change my seat? He stinks."

"I do not!" I protested.

"No one's changing their seat," Blake told him wearily.

"I'm going to be sick," Mark protested.

I jumped up and screamed, "WHAT'S WRONG WITH YOU?"

Everyone laughed.

I knew then that I'd made a colossal mistake. My voice hadn't changed yet, and it came out like a shriek. I collapsed into my chair, humiliated (and more than a little frustrated). All I was trying to do was stand up for myself.

As Mr. Blake tried to quiet the class, Mark leaned over and whispered to me, *"Such a Baby."*

I tried to shrug it off. It wasn't like we were friends, and *then* he turned on me. He never knew me to begin with. So, I tried to ignore his comments and avoided him the best I could.

I'd started it myself, and Mark ran with it. But, of course, it didn't help that he knew exactly how to provoke me, teasing me until I got mad and then laughing with his friends when I told him to stop. Or, when I tried to ignore him, he'd circle me like a vulture and wait for me to crack. It almost became a routine.

That's where the whole "immature" thing came from.

As the weeks wore on, Mark's insults became more creative, and he started recruiting his friends to join in on the fun. Before I knew it, I had a reputation. I became the daily target of crude comments ("Did you smell that?") and rumors suggesting that I cried or stomped my feet when I got upset (not true). After a while, it seemed like I was getting a verbal punch every ten minutes.

That was the crazy thing. I was mature enough to know what he was doing, but no one else could see it.

I didn't tell my mom. I wanted to handle it myself. I didn't think of it as "bullying" because I felt I had something to do with it. I figured it would be too complicated to explain.

But the ridicule that Mark had started became so common that pretty much everyone started to keep their distance from me. Whenever I thought I was making a new friend, my new reputation would scare them away. He made sure of that.

I was miserable, and I decided to confront him head-on. It would be the "mature" thing to do, I thought.

I tried to wait for just the right time, hoping to find him alone and talk to him away from other people. Unlike me, though, he'd been making friends. He always had people around him. People were friendly to me, but they didn't want to risk the possibility that I might embarrass them somehow. More than a few people told me I should "stand up to Mark."

Finally, I confronted him one day as we all waited in the hall just before Blake's class.

"I want to talk to you," I told him, trying to sound forceful.

He gave me a stupid smirk.

"So talk."

People were already watching us.

"Alone."

"ALONE?" Mark shouted it so everyone could hear.

Mr. Blake opened the door to the classroom, and we started to file in. I turned my back to Mark, deciding it was useless to try.

"Forget it."

"If you have something to say, then say it." He walked to our desk, not waiting for an answer.

I thought about ignoring him and sitting down, but then decided I should go for it.

"Why are you being like this to me?"

He sat, put his book bag down, and stared up at me for a few seconds.

With a quick glance around to make sure people were listening, He smiled and said contemptuously, "You're not going to cry, are you?"

It was *so* infuriating, but I decided to stand my ground. "Tell me."

For an instant, it seemed like he might give me a serious answer, but then he mocked me again.

"Tell me."

I heard somebody nearby giggle. I realized my attempt was useless. I sat down next to him and stared ahead at Mr. Blake's desk.

Mark and his little crowd laughed.

Now that he knew how frustrated I was, things got worse.

I'd be walking down the hall, and someone would slap me in the head as they ran by. I'd tie my shoe and get kicked in the butt.

I finally caught him alone in the school library and tried again.

"What have I ever done to you?"

He looked around for the librarian to ensure we weren't being watched and pushed me up against the shelves. He stepped closer, so I had to look up at him. At the time, he was almost a foot taller than me.

"I don't like 'pathetic,' Charlie."

"I'm not pathetic."

He gave me a sarcastic chuckle and walked away, leaving me feeling more powerless than ever. A part of me wanted to shake him and make him understand, but I let him leave.

The next day, I got kicked between the legs in a crowded hallway. I didn't know who it was, but I knew who was responsible. I found Mark at lunch at a table with his friends, and I didn't care who heard.

"Do you have to do this *every day?*"

He looked at me and smiled, "I have no idea what you're talking about."

More laughter.

"Yes, you do."

He took my desperation as a challenge. After winter break, Mark came up with the idea that every Friday should be *Charlie Day*, and it became a game for people to torment me.

Now, people didn't harass me the rest of the week, but I was hunted like an animal every Friday. I figured that was Mark's sick sense of humor.

Fridays were a hundred times worse than anything that had happened before. The assaults could come in any form: a random punch to the stomach or a half-eaten sandwich hitting me in the face out on the lunch quad. Mark and his little gang made Fridays feel like torture.

As much as I hated what was happening, I became more convinced that I'd brought everything on myself with my immaturity and awkwardness. So, I kept my mouth shut and didn't utter a word to any adult. I wanted to take care of it on my own.

But I couldn't.

On one horrible *Charlie Day*, Mark and two of his friends caught me in the restroom when I was on the toilet, grabbed me by my ankles, and pulled me out under the stall door, pants down and everything. After that experience, I stayed away from the school restrooms. That's not easy when you were as small as I was. I knew if I gave him any chance, he could be brutal.

Any *normal* person would have finally told someone.

But I wasn't normal. That was obvious to everyone.

Especially me.

I was convinced that if I told on Mark or any of his friends, *Charlie Day* would become *Charlie Week* or *Charlie Month*. I was sure of it. That's what fear does to you.

The final *Charlie Day* of the year was on the last day of school.

It was the typical stuff. Mark and his friends grabbed me and gave me a "pantsing" behind a trash dumpster near the cafeteria. Really childish stuff, but no one seemed to get it. I couldn't understand why Mark took so much pleasure in humiliating me. When they finally let me go, I pulled up everything and ran back to the safety of the lunchroom crowd.

I didn't cry.

I *never* cried.

At the end of that day, on my way down the hallway heading out of school, someone body-slammed me, driving the side of my head into a brick wall. I stood there, stunned, my hands searching above my ear for what I was sure would be a vicious lump. I was vaguely aware of kids screaming at each other, but I wasn't sure what was happening. My head was throbbing, my ears were ringing, and I saw blood when I looked at my hands.

This was far more than a Charlie Day humiliation. This took things to a whole different level.

Someone touched my arm, but I pulled away. I wasn't sure if they were trying to help or harm me, but I didn't stay to find out. I stumbled out of the building as fast as possible.

I remember walking home, my head pounding and feeling sick. I was relieved, though. At least it was *over*. Finally, I would have a couple of months to relax in peace. Then, maybe I could figure things out and come up with a better strategy.

I looked forward to reading tons of science fiction and playing video games with some of my online friends (the only ones I had). Even though they were spread all over the world, they gave me hope knowing that at least some kids enjoyed being my friend and cared what happened to me.

The first Monday after school was out, I slept late and was still lying in bed, staring at the ceiling and enjoying my freedom. Mom had been at work for hours already. I expected it would be a nice, quiet day. I hadn't told her what had happened at school. I had enough drama. School was over, anyway. I decided next year would be better.

Then someone knocked on the front door. I ignored it at first, but then they knocked again.

I scrambled to my feet, pulled my pants over my pajama bottoms, and ran to answer it.

I opened the door.

"Hey, Charlie."

Mark smiled at me like we were best friends.

3

The Visit

I started to shut the door in his face. Why wouldn't I? I hated Mark more than anyone else I'd ever met.

Why would he be at my home?

"Wait," he said, pushing past me into the apartment. I was left holding the door, unsure whether I should close it or keep it open. With my mom at work, I was on my own.

"Get out of here!" I warned him.

He smiled at me, "Relax."

"Leave!"

He folded his arms, calmly telling me, "No."

I slammed the door shut.

"What do you want?" It infuriated me that he was acting like he had a right to do anything he wanted.

"Don't be so mad."

I knew I couldn't physically throw him out.

"I bet you're glad school is out."

I swore to myself that if he tried to do something to me in my own home, I would grab something and bash him in the head. I eyed the lamp beside the door.

"Relax," he said again. He glanced down and noticed my hands balled into fists, "All ready to fight, huh?"

He was mocking me.

"This isn't a joke," I told him.

He moved past me further into the apartment.

"Where's your room?"

"LEAVE!"

He looked over his shoulder at me, unconcerned, "You know you're not going to do anything about it."

"I will!"

The door to my mom's bedroom was open, so he tried the only closed door—my bedroom.

"Why are you here?" I asked, catching up with him.

He pushed open my door.

"Stay out of my room!"

He ignored me and stepped inside.

After a few seconds of looking around, he finally turned to face me.

"You know, you're really immature."

Rage and frustration boiled through my veins, my heart hammering in my chest. I had no choice but to wait this thing out.

Whatever it was.

He nodded calmly at the bed.

"You've got, like, *five* stuffed animals. Seriously?"

He walked over to my bookshelf, ignoring all of my science fiction books, and pulled out the one picture book I still had. It was my very first favorite book.

"Kiddie books?"

"I have a lot of other books."

I snatched it back, my voice raised and defiant. "GET OUT OF HERE!"

His face burned with rage for just an instant, and I wondered if he would beat me up in my own room. Then he suddenly calmed down and shook his head.

"I'm *trying* to be your friend, Charlie."

I put the book back on the shelf.

"I don't believe you."

"Do you know why people do things to you? You know why you have no friends?"

"Because of you. Get out of here!" My voice cracked with emotion.

"I'll tell you why: Because you're immature. Because you're a baby."

I tried to physically push him back toward the door.

"GET OUT OF HERE!"

I couldn't move him, of course. In response, he thrust his finger into my chest with such force that it hurt. I stumbled back as much from shock as the force of his gesture.

"I'm trying to be nice to you, you little baby."

I could barely breathe through my rage, gasping, "*What do you want?*"

"*Maybe* I'm trying to apologize," he said, stepping back and sitting on my bed like I had invited him. "*Maybe* I'm sorry and want to be your friend."

"You're not acting like it," I told him, "and get off my bed!"

Mark shrugged and quietly asked, "What have you got to lose?"

"I hate you," I reminded him.

"I know. But what if I'm being honest?"

I didn't trust him, but I figured that if I pretended to be gullible, maybe he would finally leave.

I took a deep breath, glanced at my stuffed animals, then back at him.

"Just don't call me baby."

4

Control

Abruptly, Mark's voice softened, almost like he believed what he was saying, "I won't call you baby."

I hesitated, then said, "Thanks."

"Unless..." His voice trailed off.

"Unless?"

"Unless you act like one."

I wasn't sure if he was setting me up for some joke. But we weren't in school, and there was no one else around.

I dropped down into my desk chair and thought it over. I could argue with him or stay calm and see what happens.

"I won't," I said with more than a little reluctance.

"I mean, I *want* to be friends with you, but not if you act like a baby."

"I said I won't."

At that moment, I wasn't thinking about everything he had done to me in the past. I was just so tired of not having a friend. I wanted to believe him.

After what felt like an eternity, he finally answered, "Okay."

I breathed a sigh of relief.

"Look, it's okay." He took on his friendly tone again, "I get it. I mean, you don't have a dad. *My* dad tells me if I'm doing wrong."

"I have my mom," I pointed out.

Mark thrust his hand out, grabbed Max, my favorite stuffed animal, and held him to the light. He ran his fingers over the soft fur, inspecting every detail with a scrutinizing eye.

"Yeah, but your mom isn't always going to tell you when you're acting like a baby, is she?"

I was dying to snatch Max back, but I resisted the urge. Maybe Mark was right.

He looked at me again and asked, "What if I tell you when you're acting like a baby?"

I really wished he'd stop using that word.

I looked into Max's eyes, "That's *exactly* what you did all year."

"Well, not making fun of you this time." He started playing with Max's arms with each word, "I mean, if you act like a baby, I'll tell you, like a dad would. I'll tell you if you're acting wrong."

"You're not my dad."

"I'm a friend, though, right?"

I couldn't get my head around what was happening. I was almost sick with anxiety. But I liked that he called me a friend.

He tossed Max onto the floor like garbage.

Get him later, I told myself, keeping my eyes on Mark.

"Okay," I told him.

"I'm hungry," he said, getting up, "do you want to go out and get something?"

I nodded. This kind of offer was *huge* to me, but I knew he would think it was babyish if I seemed to care, so I stayed calm.

"We can go to Marty's," I suggested. That was a little pizza place a lot of kids went to—I knew Mark and his friends went there. I had no friends, so I never went.

But now things were different.

We headed out of my bedroom and toward the front door.

"Hold on," I told him just before we left, "I forgot my wallet."

I ran back to my bedroom and put Max back on the bed. I already had my wallet.

We walked down to Marty's, talking all the way about movies and shows. Mark was amazed that we didn't have any streaming channels. He was almost unbelievably nice to me for the first time, but I struggled not to overreact or show how happy I felt. When we got to the restaurant twenty minutes later, I felt like he might be for real—he might really want to be my friend.

We both ordered a slice and a soft drink. He had pepperoni, and I had double cheese.

"It's so good," I told him.

He took a bite of his slice.

"I really like it," I said, feeling self-conscious that he wasn't talking.

He took another bite but still didn't say anything.

"Do you like yours?" I asked.

He put his slice down on his plate and looked at me in disbelief.

"You're doing it."

I wasn't sure what he was saying, "Doing what?"

He raised his voice.

"YOU'RE ACTING LIKE A BABY."

Everyone looked at our table. I was embarrassed, but I still had no idea what I had done wrong. Or why he had to announce it to the entire restaurant.

"I'm sorry," I said to him quietly. I wondered if I was *that* bad.

He lifted his pizza slice in his hands and pointed it at me, his voice low and menacing, "Don't do it again."

I still wanted to ask what I'd done, but I didn't and stared at his pizza.

"Okay."

On the walk home, I finally risked the question, "Back there, what did I do wrong?"

We abruptly stopped walking.

His face grew red with anger, "You can't be serious."

I wanted to explain my side, but fear kept me quiet.

He shouted, "YOU WERE BEING A WHINER, YOU WERE BEGGING, YOU WERE ACTING EMBARRASSING." His words stung. He was so mad; I was worried that he had already decided he couldn't be my friend after all.

"I HATE your whiny little voice, 'how is it? Do you like yours?'" He made my voice sound all high-pitched.

"I'm sorry," I whispered.

He poked me in the chest again, "You know, my dad would be so mad if I acted like that."

"I'm sorry."

"Do you want to be my friend or not?"

I was terrified that I might have messed things up, "What?"

He spoke the words slowly as if I had trouble understanding: "Do...you...want...to...be...my...friend...or...NOT!"

"I do!" I knew I sounded desperate, but I couldn't help it. "I'm sorry."

He poked me again, "I would get punished if I acted like that."

I wasn't sure why he told me that, but it scared me, "I won't do it again, I swear."

He poked me even harder, "Better not."

We started walking again. He went back to talking about movies like nothing had happened. He was calm. I made sure to agree with everything he said.

I wanted to act *the right way* in front of him, but I could already see it wouldn't be easy.

I concluded that I deserved to be yelled at, even if other people heard it. I brought it on myself.

He was my friend, after all.

I trusted him.

5

You Really Need to Grow Up

When Mom and I ate dinner that night, I contemplated whether or not to tell her that Mark had come by. On the one hand, I knew she would be proud that I had made a friend, but I hesitated to bring it up yet because I didn't want her to be disappointed when he inevitably moved on.

I chose to keep my mouth shut.

She knew nothing about *Charlie Day* or how far on the edges I was at school. I kept it a secret. She figured I was shy and kept trying to give me "advice" about speaking up more and joining clubs—I had decided that none of it would work. She spent the whole year "encouraging" me to make friends. If I wasn't careful, she would overreact if I told her about Mark.

When Mark didn't call me in the morning, I decided I'd made the right decision not to tell her. He'd lost interest. He probably was trying to be friendly and then discovered how weak and pathetic I was.

I was still in my pajamas at one in the afternoon, watching TV in my bed, when Mark called me.

He didn't even say hi.

"Hey, you want to do something?"

"Sure," I said, a little stunned.

"Then come over," he said and hung up.

I was surprised that he'd hung up so quickly, but I decided it was a good sign that we understood each other.

I threw off my pajamas, put on a clean shirt and pants, and rushed out the door. I thought it would be funny to run over to his house, a couple of blocks away, and knock on his door much sooner than he expected. I was a pretty good runner.

"Hi!" I shouted as he opened the door. I couldn't wait to see the smile on his face.

But he didn't even crack a smile. Instead, his expression made me feel ashamed and guilty for subjecting him to my presence.

Mark stepped aside, and I went in, grateful he didn't just yell at me and send me home. I promised myself I would think harder about not acting in ways that would get him angry.

Stepping into his room, I realized how childish my own bedroom was by comparison. It wasn't only because of my collection of plush toys and a horse poster; his room had a big TV on the wall, a desktop computer, and a bookshelf twice the size of mine and crammed with books. He even had his own bathroom with a sliding door.

We played video games for a while, but he got frustrated with me because I didn't know how to use his controller, so he decided we should go down to *Village*. I thought that was probably a better idea.

Village Marketplace was nothing more than a big parking lot with a long line of random stores and fast food places, but it was the only place where a kid around here could go without asking for a ride. It would feel less awkward than sitting around in Mark's bedroom. And it was a couple of miles away, so we would have a lot of time to talk along the way.

First, he talked about superhero movies, which I knew very little about, and asked me if I watched a couple of shows he liked until he remembered that I didn't have any streaming services. I got a little nervous that he would find me boring if I had nothing to say, so I randomly asked about his favorite food.

"Pizza, what's yours?"

"Pizza." It was actually Chinese food, but I wanted to show him we had something in common, so we talked about pizza for a while. I asked him who makes the best pizza, and then we spoke about cheesy bread.

I was feeling good about the walk down to the stores. I was getting better at having the right kind of conversation with Mark, and I felt like he was really becoming a good friend. So I decided right then that I would tell my mom that night when she came home from work.

We walked under the huge *Village Marketplace* sign at the parking lot entrance and headed for the electronics store straight ahead. As soon as we got inside, we separated. I went to the right toward the computers, and he went somewhere to the left.

I looked at a gaming laptop that I knew was so expensive that all I could do was dream about it, but it was still fun to play with it and admire the big hi-def screen. My old laptop was about as far from gaming as you can get.

Suddenly, Mark grabbed me by my arm, "Let's get out!"

He was mad, but I was sure it wasn't about me.

Once we were back outside, he yelled at me, "YOU DID IT AGAIN!"

"I was just looking at laptops," I protested.

"Do you want to be friends with me or not?"

"Yes, but—"

"Then stop acting like a baby!"

I thought about arguing, but I knew already that it was more important to calm him down first.

"I'm sorry," I told him, without knowing what I was apologizing for.

Instantly, Mark's anger disappeared, "Let's get something to eat."

We walked over to the frozen yogurt place for a snack. I'd been there before with my mom; you choose the flavors you want and add your own toppings. I was careful not to start chattering about it, though, in case he thought I was acting immature again. He wasn't being very talkative, so I felt I had to be extra careful.

Usually, I would combine the strawberry, peanut butter, and vanilla flavors, but Mark went for chocolate and double chocolate. I did the same and added peanuts as one of the toppings. Also, he added caramel sauce instead of fudge, and I did that too.

A minute after we sat down, he said, "I'm sorry I got mad at you."

"It's okay."

"But you know why, right?"

That was a tricky question, so I shrugged as if my mouth was full and I couldn't talk (it wasn't).

"It's because you act immature sometimes, and it's embarrassing."

"Sorry." I still didn't know what I'd done, but I felt guilty.

"We're friends, right?" he asked.

I nodded.

"Yeah."

He smiled and swallowed another spoonful of yogurt, "My dad would get *so* mad if I acted like you."

I wasn't sure what I should say, so I dug into my yogurt to keep busy.

"If I tell you that you're acting like a baby, it's only so that you'll know."

"Okay."

"It's not like I *want* to be mean. You just need to grow up."

I stared into my yogurt, "I know."

"Look at me," he said, and I did. He was smiling, "Repeat after me."

I was thinking, *I don't like this,* but I decided to stay quiet.

"Say, 'I promise not to act like a baby.'"

My cheeks felt hot as I watched him. Why was he doing this, especially out in the open?

"Say it."

People were at the next table, so I muttered, "I promise not to act like a baby."

"Louder."

"I get it, okay?"

He just stared and waited. I figured I brought it on myself, so I said it a little louder, "I promise not to act like a baby."

"Say that you promise not to embarrass me."

I wondered how horrible I had acted to make him feel like he had to do this. I looked around to make sure no one was listening.

"I promise not to embarrass you."

He finished the last of his yogurt, licked his spoon, and thought a moment before adding, "Say that you won't act like a two-year-old that pooped his diaper."

That was over the line.

"WHY are you doing this?"

He glared at me but didn't answer.

"I'm not saying that," I told him, but I couldn't look him in the eye.

"If you don't like it, don't act like a baby. I'm teaching you a lesson."

He was done with his yogurt, so he got up and started heading out, leaving his empty cup on the table. I got up and followed him, still carrying mine. I was only half done.

"Throw it away," he ordered me, "you'll just drip it all over yourself."

Reluctantly, I threw it away. I still thought he was being overly harsh, though.

But at least I showed him I had my limits.

6

Things Get Complicated

That night, I finally told my mom about Mark, but I didn't mention that he thought I was immature and bossed me around. I still figured that was all my fault, and I had to deal with it and make it better.

"Why don't you invite him over for dinner on Friday?"

The idea instantly made me nervous, "I'm not sure if he'll be able to."

"Of course, he will. I'll call his parents."

"He might be busy," I said, hoping it was true.

"Then we'll make it another night."

I called Mark, stuttering with panic. "M-m-my mom is inviting you to dinner at our house."

He responded immediately with a confident "sure," sending my heart beating faster. Then he put his Mom on the phone with my mom, and I tried to move close enough to hear every word they said about me.

She told Mark's mom I was "excited" to have a friend like Mark and even told her I had trouble making friends. Then she went all-in on embarrassment and said that Mark might be a "good example" for me and joked about how I needed boys to "show him the way."

I hoped that Mark wasn't standing as close to his mom as I was and could hear what my mom was saying.

He already thought I was a baby; this would convince him once and for all.

My anxiety was going through the roof, so once the call was over, I returned to my room and cuddled up with Max. Then I realized I was acting babyish and threw him across the room like Mark had.

I didn't see Mark again until Friday, which gave me plenty of time to panic that I would mess up. I made sure my mom ordered a pepperoni pizza and cheesy bread so that Mark could have his favorite food.

On Friday, Mark showed up just after five and gave me two rolled-up posters. One was a hot car, and the other was some manga thing I didn't know anything about.

"You need new posters," he told me.

"Thanks."

My mom thanked him, too, and then immediately asked me if I thanked him, which was embarrassing. At least he could see me standing up to her and telling her that I did already.

I had hoped that just Mark and I would eat together, but my mom wanted to join us, and all three of us sat down at the kitchen table.

Right away, she started telling Mark what she said to his mom—that I was happy to have a friend. Worse, she actually added, "I know he can be a little immature sometimes, but kids should give him a chance."

I was too shocked to say anything. I could hardly believe that she would actually say that to Mark.

He smirked, "Yeah, he is a little immature."

"You're going to be a big help to him."

"Mom, please," I pleaded as quietly as possible.

"She's *just* trying to help," Mark told me, his voice already hinting at the sarcasm that always signaled his rising anger. I decided I shouldn't say anything else.

"Anyway, I'll help him," he assured her.

He was a month younger than me, yet my mom talked to Mark like he was another adult.

"Oh, I forgot!" He didn't even glance at me, "Can Charlie sleep at my house tomorrow?"

Mark hadn't mentioned a sleepover; I would have devised an excuse if I had known. Too many things could go wrong, and the whole thing seemed potentially humiliating. Even though I was thirteen, I had never been to a sleepover, and the idea of being in pajamas around Mark filled me with dread.

"I'm sure he'd love to!"

To say anything at this point would have seemed babyish, so I just forced, "Cool," and left it at that.

"Cool," Mark didn't make it so obvious, but I knew he was mocking me.

I figured that he already knew I would mess up.

7

Anxiety

I didn't sleep much that night.

I worked out a plan to wake up "sick" in the morning so mom wouldn't let me go. I was good at pretending to be sick. I'd used that strategy a few times growing up—and recently to avoid *Charlie Day*.

It was standard little-kid stuff. I'd get dressed and sit down for breakfast like usual, but act extra tired and eat very slowly. She would ask if I was okay, and I shrugged and—this was important—answered her with a dazed, "I guess so."

She would do the old *check my forehead* trick, and even though I was perfectly fine, she would be unsure and tell me we "shouldn't take any chances" and that I should sleep it off. It worked as long as I didn't try it too often.

Unfortunately, school was over for the summer, and this was Saturday morning. Mom didn't have to rush off to work. She knew I was nervous about the sleepover, so she was immediately suspicious. When I dragged myself into the kitchen, she didn't bother putting her hand on my forehead. Instead, she talked to me like I was a toddler.

"I know you're worried about the sleepover, but it's going to be okay."

"I'm not worried," I lied, trying to sell the act and be sincere, "I just feel exhausted." Finally, I sighed to give my story some extra drama.

If I'm completely honest, I knew I was being immature about it, but the fear was overwhelming.

"There's nothing to be nervous about. Mark's a good kid."

"I'm *really* tired," I said, picking at my scrambled eggs and looking right at her.

Then she said something that gutted me.

"Charlie, you're not acting very mature."

"But I'm tired," I tried one last time. I already knew it was useless, though.

Mark was right. Mom was right. I was fooling no one.

I was acting like a baby.

I gave up the fight and accepted that I'd definitely be going to his sleepover.

I spent the rest of the morning and early afternoon in panic mode. I prepared my backpack with a change of clothes and pajamas several hours before I needed to leave and then watched television to pass the time.

Mark had told me to be there at four o'clock because we were going out to dinner for Chinese food, which I thought was an excellent idea.

He called me twice during the day about our plans for the night, but I was afraid to call him myself in case he thought I was acting too babyish and excited.

Still, I was so worried that I felt like I was having an anxiety attack. I lay on my bed and took a few deep breaths to remind myself not to overreact

I wanted to avoid making a fool of myself, saying the wrong thing, or talking too much. I promised myself that I would agree with everything that Mark wanted. I wanted this to go smoothly, so he and Mom saw I was more mature than they thought.

8

The Shower

The closer it came to 4 p.m., the more my anxiety grew. Mark's house was just a ten-minute walk, but I became obsessed with calculating when to knock on his door. Mark had said to be there at four, but what should I do? Should I knock a few minutes before or a few minutes after? Should I knock as soon as my watch displayed four?

I was worried that I would seem too excited if I knocked too early. Too late, and he might think I wasn't listening to him.

I finally decided to knock at 4 p.m. but to wait for maybe thirty seconds, so it wasn't precisely when the time changed. Hopefully, that would be okay. I thought it was a good possibility that he would be watching the time to see what I might do and if I was going to do something embarrassing and childish again. So far, whenever we got together, I felt he was judging me at every moment.

I needed to get it right.

I reviewed the contents of my backpack one last time and started walking down to Mark's house. I moved slowly because I didn't want to get there too early and have to wait outside for the right time. That would have felt awkward and weird and even worse if he saw me. So I slowed down at the corner just before turning onto Mark's street and pretended to inspect a crack in the sidewalk until the timing was right.

I felt scared but told myself that I was overreacting. I was doing what ten million other kids did every day. I was walking to a friend's house. Just because I hadn't done it a lot didn't mean it wasn't the most normal thing in the world.

"Calm down," I whispered to myself, adding *don't act like a baby* in my head.

Somehow, that made me feel better. I walked up to the door and knocked. Right away, Mark answered.

"Hey, Charlie!" He was friendly like he was actually happy to see me. His parents came to the door too, and they were really nice. His dad shook my hand. As weird as it sounds, I never had strangers act so happy to see me.

His dad looked at his watch and said, "We'll leave for the restaurant in about an hour. You guys can chill for now."

We walked into Mark's bedroom, and I dropped my backpack on the floor. He had a game up on his PC, so I walked over.

"What are you playing?"

Instead of answering, he asked me, "Did you shower before you came here?"

That was an odd question. I thought it was a joke. I shrugged and laughed, "Well, last night."

"Last night?"

Suddenly, he wasn't smiling anymore.

I shrugged and joked, "I'm clean, you know!"

He stared at me and didn't say anything.

"What's wrong?"

He pointed at the bathroom, "Take a shower."

"Very funny." I laughed again. He made zero sense. It wasn't like I smelled or anything. It was just plain weird.

But he was serious, "If you don't, you're going home."

Now it was my turn to stare.

"Do it," he ordered.

"I took one last night," I insisted. In school, he'd randomly tease me about the same thing without any reason at all. Now he was doing it again.

"Maybe you don't understand this because you're kind of *immature*." He emphasized the word. "But you should take a shower before you come to someone's house to go out with their family."

I felt sick to my stomach. I really didn't want to take a shower in his house. It just seemed too private.

But I also wondered if I was being immature.

He picked up his phone and showed it to me, "You want to ask your mommy?"

"No."

I decided to give in and get it done as fast as possible.

He threw his phone back on his desk, "Hurry up and take a shower."

I went over to his bathroom, sliding the door shut behind me. It had no lock.

The shower wasn't like mine, which had a plastic curtain. Instead, this one was like a rich person's shower, with glass all around.

I thought for a second about telling him I would run back to my own house to shower, but I was sure he would think I was being a baby. My mom would probably think so, too.

I took off my shoes and my socks.

I was shaking with humiliation but told myself, "Stop this." I was still trembling when I took off my shirt.

Why was he doing this? I didn't want to ruin the sleepover by complaining, but it seemed unfair. Next time, I would make sure to take a shower before I did anything with him, but I suspected he was doing this just to push me around. Next time, I promised myself I wouldn't give in so easily.

I looked at the door again to ensure I'd closed it, then took my pants and underwear off. Then, I turned on the shower and got in.

How long would he think was long enough? I didn't want to be in there for long, but I didn't want him to think I was faking a shower, either. We still had almost an hour until we left, so I reminded myself for probably the tenth time that day that I'd better calm myself down, take a regular shower, and not rush things.

I poured some shampoo and had just started washing my hair when I heard the door slide open. I looked over my shoulder.

Mark had walked in.

"Why are you in here?" I stepped to the far side of the shower. Since the walls were all glass, there was no privacy. I hated that could see my bare butt.

"Relax, you little baby. I was just bringing you a towel."

I stared at the shower nozzle but didn't hear him leave.

"You can leave, Mark."

I looked over my shoulder, and he was still standing there.

"How about a thank you?"

"Thank you," I said quickly, "You can leave now."

He laughed at me and returned to the bedroom, leaving the door open.

"Please close the door," I shouted as nicely as possible.

He ignored me, of course. He sat at his desk, playing a video game. There was no way for me to close the door without stepping out of the shower.

I was sure that he intentionally left it open to embarrass me.

I took a deep breath and whispered my calming words again, trying to keep myself from losing it.

"Stop this."

9

The Sleepover

When I was ready to get out of the shower, I discovered that Mark had returned to the bathroom, combing his hair in the mirror. The towel he'd brought in for me was on the counter right next to him, far out of my reach.

I decided that asking him to hand it to me because I was shy about being naked might get him angry again, so I covered myself with one hand, stepped out of the shower, and grabbed the towel.

I turned my back to Mark and began drying off.

"Have you ever been to Chang's?" he asked me. He didn't sound angry anymore.

"No, never."

"It's great. Best Chinese food ever. You're going to love the orange chicken. Also, you have to try the spare ribs. And the chicken fried rice. Well, everything."

He was taking forever to comb his hair and inspect his face. I had hoped to wait until he left the bathroom to put on my clothes, but it was clear he wasn't going anytime soon. I wrapped the towel around my waist and joined him at the counter. Right away, he handed me his hairbrush. He kept talking.

"We're not into shrimp fried rice in this family, so you're out of luck if you want that! But seriously, everything else is incredible."

"I like wonton soup," I added, not wanting to stand there quietly and look awkward.

"Definitely the wonton soup," he agreed, nodding happily, "I love the wonton soup! But, hey, you better hurry up and get dressed. We have to leave soon!"

Clearly, I wouldn't be allowed to dress privately, so I gave up on the idea. Instead, I grabbed my underwear, turned away from him, and slipped them on while letting the towel fall, preserving a little privacy.

"I hope you're hungry!" he continued.

"I am," I joked, pulling on my pants like I was used to dressing in front of another person.

I was relieved that he wasn't mad at me anymore.

So far, so good.

Dinner was fantastic, and Mark didn't lecture, glare at, or nudge me even once.

His parents were extremely nice, and I got to tell them about my aunt's horse, and they seemed genuinely interested. Of course, I didn't know all that much about it, but that didn't seem to matter. Mark asked about the horse, too, and wanted to know what it was like to ride it. I haven't yet because it's a big horse and I'm small, and I'm still nervous about it. I didn't want to say all that, so I just said it was great.

All the food was as good as Mark said it would be, and I was so stuffed I felt like my stomach was twice its size. When he came with me to the restaurant bathroom, I thought maybe he was doing it because he wanted to criticize me privately, but he just peed.

***

We walked around for a while after dinner, and it was pretty late by the time we got back to the house. Our original plan was to watch movies all night, but we both wanted to sleep. I pulled my pajamas out of my backpack, but he grabbed them out of my hand and stuffed them back in.

I had to laugh, "What are you doing?"

He laughed, too, "Babies wear pajamas."

"Mark, lots of people wear pajamas. You're being silly."

"Silly's a baby word." He didn't seem mad, but I wasn't sure how serious he was. He took off his pants, then hopped into bed in his boxers.

I stood there, feeling stupid. I didn't want to sleep in my underwear, but I didn't want to overreact. So I decided to sleep without pajamas and took off my pants.

"We gotta get you boxers," he said, a comment that made me feel even more uncomfortable. I hopped into the sleeping bag he'd laid on the floor and pulled off my shirt once I tucked myself in. I had to work on some things to stop being immature, but I felt I was improving.

I still felt like he was bossing me around, though.

***

When I woke up the next morning, Mark was already in the shower. I sat up and rubbed my eyes, still half in the sleeping bag. He left the bathroom door open again. I figured he wouldn't mind if I went in and peed, but as much as he didn't mind doing things like that, that was a little too much for me. So, I decided to wait until he was out.

He turned off the shower, dried off, and returned to the bedroom with the towel around his waist.

"Your turn."

I got up, grabbed my stuff, and headed for the bathroom.

"You're taking a shower, right?"

"You and showers," I joked.

But then he blocked me.

"Take a shower," he told me.

I was honest with him finally, "You're being weird."

He grabbed my backpack and pants and said, "You're not getting your clothes until you shower."

"I'll take one when I get home; what's your problem?" I didn't mind that I sounded angry. He had no reason to make a big thing out of it. I tried to grab my pants back, but he wouldn't let them go.

"Do it now."

He had flipped into full *mean* mode again.

I felt so helpless and stupid that I couldn't figure him out and understand if he was being unfair or if I was being immature.

Finally, I gave up and went into the bathroom in just my underwear. At least he let me close the door this time.

10

Lucky Me

I didn't tell Mom about the weird stuff with the showers. I still needed to figure out whether I'd done anything wrong or if Mark was trying to tell me something I was too stupid to understand. But I couldn't bear the thought of Mom telling me, *I've been meaning to talk to you about your hygiene.*

So I kept quiet.

Mark and I mainly had a good time. He was okay when he wasn't trying to control everything.

I told Mom about Mark's parents, how nice they were to me, and our discussion about the horse. It made her happy, so I felt less weird about the shower. Mom suggested that Mark might want to come with us the next time we went out to my aunt's ranch. That idea made me a little anxious because it practically guaranteed that I would finally have to ride the horse (and not chicken out like I always did).

She told me how happy she was for me and how lucky I was to find a good friend. She was proud of me, she said. She was so "supportive" that it made me feel like she was surprised that I wasn't the loser she thought I was. She made me feel like I was some random kid who was lucky to be Mark's friend instead of her son. I wanted to tell her to give it a break.

But I didn't.

I was so worn out from the stress of the sleepover that I slept late Monday morning. I ate breakfast, watched a little television, and was still in pajamas at eleven o'clock when someone knocked at the door.

Well, "someone" isn't entirely true. I knew at the first knock that it had to be Mark. Sooner or later, I wanted to tell him to call before he came over.

He held back a laugh, looking over my pajamas, "Those are worse than the other ones!"

The pajamas I was wearing had pictures of horses. They were made for younger kids, but since I was small, Mom bought them for me. I didn't mind wearing them, either; they were comfy.

This time, I stood up for myself and tried to make a little joke out of it, "Well, it's my house, my rules. And anyway, it's not like I'm going to answer the door in my underwear!"

He laughed, and I counted that as a small victory. I promised myself to talk to him eventually about his other weirdness.

"Do you have plastic bags?" he asked, walking past me into the apartment.

I thought that was a super random question, but I went to a kitchen cabinet and showed him where they were.

He pulled out one of the large trash bags, "You want to go to *Village* again?"

I shrugged. "Just gotta get ready," I told him, adding, "I'm going to take a shower." Of course, I was going to anyway, but knowing how interested he seemed to be in my shower habits, I thought I would let him know. Our bathroom had a lock, at least, so that would cut down on his weirdness.

I grabbed my clothes from my room and went to take a shower.

I was in the bathroom for about fifteen minutes before I returned to my bedroom.

"I made some improvements," he told me.

The horse poster was gone, replaced with the two posters he'd brought for me the other day. And my bed was missing the stuffed animals.

Including Max.

"Where are they?"

"Look," he said quietly, stepping closer to me so that I felt smaller (I was beginning to see that as a regular Mark trick), "I knew you wouldn't do it on your own, so I got rid of them for you."

"Got rid of them?" I went over to the closet to find them.

"I threw them out," he told me, "sometimes you have to be tough about it."

Maybe he was partly right; truthfully, I didn't care anymore about the other animals. But Max was different.

"Where?" I looked around the room for the plastic bag, but it was nowhere in sight. I headed for my bedroom door.

He blocked me.

"Don't be a baby about it."

He didn't sound angry—but I was filled with rage.

"You had no right to do that!"

"Would you have done it yourself?"

I didn't answer him.

"They're in the dumpster, so they're as good as gone. So let's go."

The dumpster!

I wanted to look for Max immediately, but with Mark, I knew I had to play this carefully. Part of me knew that getting upset about stuffed animals would tick him off.

I reminded myself that Mark didn't know about Max—the only thing I owned that had any connection to my father. Mom said they both gave it to me for my second birthday, three months before he died. To Mark, it was just a ratty bear.

The trash truck had already stopped by early in the morning, which meant the dumpster wouldn't be emptied again until tomorrow. That meant I could rescue Max when I got home.

I almost felt sick to my stomach, but I didn't do anything.

I would just have to wait and deal with it later.

"Sure, let's go," I told Mark, forcing myself to sound unconcerned. I already wanted to get back from the stores as soon as possible.

Unlike the last time we went, he didn't get mad at me even once during the whole time or call me a baby. When we went to the frozen yogurt place again, he didn't push me to finish. He finally seemed to be okay with me, which felt good.

Despite what he'd done to Max.

After lunch, I told him I had some chores as an excuse to go home. As soon as we parted at the corner where I went to the left, and he went straight, I started running.

When I got back to our building, I headed straight for the dumpster. It was already piled high with plastic bags like the one I'd given to Mark.

I didn't care. I climbed into the bin and started ripping them open, looking for Max and all the others. I had to dive deeper to hide when people came by to throw in more garbage. It took me half an hour of ripping into bags of rotten food and dirty diapers until I finally found my animals.

I was covered in grime, baby poop, and every other gross thing, but at least I found my bear. Maybe I *was* acting like a baby, but Max was safe.

11

The Experiment

I spent an hour in the shower before I could get rid of the stomach-churning dumpster smell. I had to wash my hair five or six times.

In school, Mark and his friends had made me feel entirely alone, and I lived in fear, but at least I understood the reality of my life. I was the least liked, most hated, and most rejected kid. But, weirdly, I knew what to expect. It was predictable. But I also knew I could come home every day, and my mom would be there to pour on the—I might as well admit it—mothering. I would almost have laid on the couch and sucked my thumb if she wouldn't have thought that I was completely crazy. And for the extra tough days, I had Max to cuddle up with and hide under my covers in bed.

Now, everything was confusing. Mark might have been rude about it, but he wasn't entirely wrong about getting rid of my stuffed animals. Especially since we had become friends, I already felt like I was getting too old to have all of them on my bed. What thirteen-year-old cuddles up with a teddy bear?

I thought Mark was becoming extra friendly to me now because I wasn't putting up a big fight about everything. Sometimes I protested, of course, but I also dropped things pretty quickly. I was trying to be cool about it, so he was cool with me.

So, when I stepped out of the shower and put on clean clothes, I didn't put any stuffed animals back on my bed. Instead, I put them all into a clean plastic bag—including Max—and shoved them up on the shelf in my closet behind a bunch of junk. They were still close, but they weren't obvious anymore.

I loved Mark's posters, though I was still angry he'd ruined my horse poster. It was crumbled up on the bottom of my closet. Unfortunately, there wasn't anything I could do about it now.

Despite everything, I did like how my room was coming along. It was starting to feel less like it belonged to the weird kid and more like a teenager's room.

I started feeling guilty about cutting my time short with Mark because of Max and thought up an excuse to call him.

"Hey, where did you get those posters you gave me?"

He told me he had a whole bunch of them in his closet, and I could take what I wanted.

"You could come now if you want."

It was already 4:30, but my mom wouldn't be home for a few more hours, so I headed to his house. After my super-long shower, I wasn't worried about his odd shower rule.

His parents were both at work, so it was just the two of us. He took me upstairs to his room and opened the double doors to the closet. He turned on the light and pointed toward the back, where a bunch of rolled-up posters were sticking out of an open box.

"I can take anything?"

"I'm not using them."

"Nice."

I stepped into the back of the closet and started looking at them.

That's when he started his "joke."

He shut the double doors and turned off the light.

"Very funny."

I pushed at the doors, but he'd tied them together with something, so they would only swing out an inch or two. I could see him smiling at me.

"Very funny. Let me out."

I hated being trapped and already felt my heart beating fast, but I didn't want him to think it bothered me.

He just looked at me and didn't say anything.

"Joke's over. Let me out."

"No, it's not."

"Seriously, Mark. This isn't funny. Why are you doing this?"

"It's an experiment."

"I don't like it. Let me out."

"No."

He stepped back from the closet, watching me with his arms folded.

I pushed against the doors, hoping to force them wide enough for me to squeeze through.

"I don't like this; come on."

"Nope."

"Let me out."

"Nope."

He was being stubborn for no reason at all. I guessed he was trying to see if he could get me to panic, so I kept taking deep breaths and concentrated on waiting him out—the same way I coped when he humiliated me in school. He couldn't keep me in there forever. His parents had to come home eventually.

I looked at my watch. It was just barely five o'clock. My mom wouldn't be home for an hour and a half. I wasn't sure when Mark's parents would be home.

He sat down on his bed, staring at the closet.

"Why do you think this is funny?"

Despite my best efforts, my voice cracked with stress. Now he knew I was getting upset.

He didn't say a word. Instead, he folded his arms as if he had no intention of letting me out anytime soon.

I pressed my face against the crack, pushing the doors as wide as I could manage, "At least tell me why you're doing this."

He got up from the bed and walked back to the closet.

I figured he was ready to let out.

Instead, he tightened whatever tied the two doorknobs together so the doors couldn't open at all. All I had left now was a tiny sliver of light.

I'd had enough. I pounded on the doors with my fists, "LET ME OUT!" I pounded again, throwing in a few curse words that would have given him plenty of excuses to kick my butt if we were in school.

I couldn't see his face anymore, and he said nothing else. Instead, he turned off the light, and I heard him leave the room.

I pounded again and even threw my whole body against the doors, "THERE'S SOMETHING SERIOUSLY WRONG WITH YOU!"

Now I was feeling real panic.

"LET ME OUT!"

I threw my body against the doors again.

"LET ME OUT!"

I put my shoulder into it and tried to force the door.

Finally, he returned to his room, turned on the light, and untied the door.

The second I was free, I headed out of the bedroom. He blocked me.

"GET OUT OF MY WAY!" I screamed.

"Calm down."

I tried to get past him, but he held me back.

"YOU'RE CRAZY! GET OUT OF MY WAY! YOU DON'T DO THAT TO SOMEONE!"

I was almost crying. I didn't care what he thought.

"I'm sorry, okay?" He was still blocking me, and I was still struggling to escape. "It was meant to be a joke."

"It wasn't to me!" I told him.

"I'm sorry," he repeated, quieter this time. His apology calmed me down a little bit.

I took a couple of deep breaths, trying to control my breathing and steady my emotions.

"Don't do it again!" I warned him.

He put his hands down at his sides and said, "If you're mad, you can hit me, as hard as you want, anywhere."

"I'm not going to hit you," I told him.

I wanted to, but I wasn't stupid. I couldn't do anything to him if I wanted to, and I'm not the kind of kid that hurts people. Plus, I was starting to forgive him already.

"Just don't do it again."

He pulled the posters all the way out of the closet so I could look at them in the open and choose what I wanted.

My hands were still shaking. I wondered if he noticed.

12

A Good Friend

Most of the time, Mark was okay. He could be pushy sometimes—real pushy—but he could also be a good friend. He gave me five posters and even my mom noticed how good my room looked. You're supposed to accept friends for who they are and not criticize them for the little things. After all, he was friends with me, and that couldn't be easy.

The closet thing was only for a few minutes, and I probably should have laughed it off. I did, actually, after I calmed down. He was probably right not to let me run off like I wanted.

Still, at the right time, I wanted to talk to him about how it made me feel. He'd have to be in the right mood to listen, though. I was getting better at managing his bad attitudes. He usually liked to control where we ate lunch or what movie we would watch (we started getting into a routine of watching movies at his house nearly every afternoon). But Mark would still put me in embarrassing situations—we went to a store just because he still thought wearing briefs was childish and insisted I buy new underwear. But as weird as he could make me feel sometimes, I went along with his stranger moments.

I did everything I could to make sure I didn't act immature around him, and I made sure (even though I still thought he was being unreasonable) to shower right before I went to his house. I didn't even dry my hair, so it would still be wet when I got there.

Mark's parents invited my mom and me out to dinner the following weekend, which made me nervous but was also cool. They talked about how much they liked me, how much Mark liked me, and how smart I was, and Mom told them pretty much the same about Mark. We sat there and just had to laugh at everything they said. I even whispered to Mark, "If they only knew how bad we really are!"

When we got home that night, my mom asked me something I hadn't considered.

"Do you ever see his other friends?"

I knew all of them from school, of course. They were part of his gang, the same people who had helped him make my life a nightmare. I hated all of them.

David.

Jordan.

Andrew.

I hadn't seen them during the summer, and I didn't think about asking Mark. I didn't want to see his friends. The more I thought about it, though, I realized that with the tons of time he and I spent together, he wouldn't have any time to see them.

"Maybe they're not around," I suggested, though I realized immediately that it didn't make any sense that all three of his friends were busy all summer.

It seemed strange, but I didn't want to know where they were. Mark was getting to be okay with me, and I wasn't sure what would happen if Jordan and the others started coming around. So I decided not to mention them at all.

He came over most mornings without telling me, and I made a point of answering the door in my pajamas. I finally convinced him I could do what I wanted in my own home, and he stopped criticizing me. At his sleepovers, though, he said it was a rule not to wear pajamas, just like having to shower in the morning (when he always made a point of invading my privacy). That's the only time he mentioned his other friends, telling me that sometimes all three of them were in the bathroom at the same time, and nobody cared about anybody being naked because "we're all guys."

"Well, I'm more private," I explained—but he still ignored me. He even walked into the bathroom when I was pooping once to tease me because he knew I wouldn't like it. I rolled my eyes at him and stared him down until he got bored and went back into the bedroom and watched TV. I never got angry at that sort of thing anymore, accepting it as just part of his weirdness. He had no boundaries, but I think he was starting to get the point:

I had my weirdness, and he had his weirdness.

So, I wasn't worried when Mark and his parents invited me to come up with them to their cabin in the mountains for a 3-day weekend. I thought it would be fun.

I knew how to handle him now.

13

I'm in Charge

Mark and his parents came by in their big SUV before dawn on Friday morning. The trip to the mountains would take four hours. I was up an hour before my mom to get ready, which had to be a first.

I felt good about the weekend, like Mark and I had gotten past all the awkwardness, and we were on equal footing now. And I'd never been to the mountains before, so I thought this would be an amazing weekend.

Other than trips with my mom, I'd never been away from home for three days. I would be part of Mark's family—like I was Mark's brother.

I threw my backpack in with all their supplies and got in next to Mark. The truck was big enough for his mom and dad to listen to their music and news up front, and we could talk in the back.

"I guess you and I are brothers for the weekend!" I told him. He laughed.

"And you know what?" I asked, playfully nudging him.

"What?'

"I'm a month older than you, which makes *me* the big brother."

He glanced over at me, looking me up and down as if seeing me for the first time, "But you *look* like a little brother."

I used to get mad at short jokes, but I was over it. If there was one thing that Mark had taught me, it was not to take everything so seriously.

"Well, I'm the real big brother, so I'm in charge," I joked.

"I'm in charge," he said.

"The big brother is always in charge," I said, "so you better not make me mad."

He didn't say anything for a moment, but then he leaned over and repeated, "I'm in charge."

I looked over at him, sure he was joking.

But he had stopped smiling.

Suddenly, I was sitting next to weird Mark again.

He sat up straight and looked out the window on his side.

"You're joking, right?"

He ignored me.

I wanted to tell him off, but I didn't want to trigger an argument with his parents being close by.

We didn't talk for a while. I looked out the window as the sun slowly rose. Mark had his earbuds on and was listening to music. My mom still hadn't gotten me a phone, but I didn't mind. She couldn't afford it, and I knew about cyberbullying. I didn't need a phone.

I hoped this was one of those times when he got his weirdness out of his system and returned to being friendly again.

After driving for an hour, we stopped for breakfast at a fast food place. Then, just as I thought, everything seemed to be back to normal, and Mark told me about the hiking trails near the cabin and how we could hike for miles.

"We can spend the whole day just following the trails and circling the lake."

"Just bring your lunch," his dad added, which made Mark and his mom laugh. I figured it was some inside joke between them.

When we got up to leave, I headed for the bathroom. Mark went with me. When I opened the door, I realized it was a small, single-person restroom. I was about to tell him I would go first, but instead, he pushed us inside and closed the door.

"What are you doing? It's for one person!"

He locked the door.

"What are you doing?"

He got in my face again.

"I'm in charge," he told me.

"I was trying to be funny," I told him, "Get out and let me go to the bathroom."

Instead, he went ahead and peed, then washed his hands.

"Now leave so I can go to the bathroom."

He confronted me again, "You can go when we get up there."

"That makes no sense. I have to go now. Stop being weird."

"I'm in charge," he repeated.

"Fine, you're in charge. Can I pee now?"

"I said, wait until we get up there."

Someone knocked on the door.

"Why are you being like this? We're not going to get there for hours. You can't control when I go to the bathroom!"

"I'm in charge. Or do you want me to tell my parents you're too much of a baby and want to go home?"

The person knocked again.

"Well, I'll tell your parents you won't let me pee," I told him.

"No, you won't. Let's get back to the car."

He opened the door and pushed me out in front of him as the kid who was waiting rushed in past us.

"I'm in charge," he whispered again.

There was no reason for either of us to be in charge, and he knew it. But, somehow, he forgot that I wasn't the same person I was at the beginning of summer. I wasn't just going to follow his orders.

We walked back to the car, where his parents were already waiting. I held back, letting Mark get in on his side, and then said to his parents, "I'll be right back; I have to go to the bathroom."

It would have been awkward for him to get out again and run after me, so he stayed where he was. I'm sure he was shooting one of his death stares at me, but I didn't look back.

It felt good to defy him.

When I returned to the car, he glared at me as he had in school when he wanted to scare me.

But I wasn't scared anymore.

I promised myself that I wouldn't let him push me around.

Not this weekend.

And never again.

14

Liar

Mark didn't talk to me for almost an hour. Eventually, his mom noticed and asked if everything was okay, and he gave her a sarcastic look like she didn't know anything.

He glanced over at me every once in a while but looked away as soon as I noticed. He was purposely trying to annoy me, and he was succeeding.

I knew I didn't deserve his attitude. I wondered if he planned on doing this for the entire weekend. Why would he invite me if he was going to act like this?

As the sun climbed higher in the sky, we rolled into the village of Miller Lake. The main street was crammed with souvenir shops and antique stores. They were all old-fashioned wooden storefronts, like a modern Western town. The *Miner's Kitchen* restaurant stood at one corner like an old log cabin. It wasn't too big, and it was crowded. I wondered if it was the only restaurant in town. We were seated at a small round table in the middle of the cramped space. It was just big enough for the four of us. Unfortunately, Mark was sitting directly across from me.

He tried desperately to stare me down. I wanted to tell him that for someone who called me immature, his immaturity was off the scale.

But instead, I kept quiet.

I could tell he was annoyed that he had to look at me, but I was secretly happy.

"How much has Mark told you about the cabin?" his dad asked, oblivious to our silent showdown.

"I don't know," I answered, sounding as polite as possible. "Just that it's there, I guess."

"It's a bit primitive," his mom added.

"Primitive?"

Finally, Mark spoke up with his typical sarcasm, "So basically, you're gonna have to take a crap outside."

His dad quickly corrected him, "We have an outhouse."

"The cabin isn't that bad," his mom assured me, "the main thing is that there's no heating, so you have to bundle up under blankets at night—it gets cold."

"Yeah," Mark agreed, then asked me with an exaggerated little-kid whine, "Did you bring your baby pajamas? It'll keep you warm."

I glared at him and didn't answer—but his dad finally realized what was happening.

"Okay, boys, this has got to stop."

Boys? Didn't he realize that this was one hundred percent *Mark?*

"What's going on with you two?" his mom asked.

Mark rolled his eyes at her, "We're just joking around." He looked back at me, squinting again in one of his warning glares, "Isn't that right, Charlie?"

I didn't answer him. His parents already knew the truth. They didn't believe him, and that was satisfying enough.

But then they looked at me, and his mom asked, "What's going on, Charlie?"

I wasn't planning on saying anything—this was between Mark and me. But I looked at him; he was still trying to intimidate me with his pathetic death glare, and I wasn't going to fall for it anymore.

Charlie is in charge of Charlie.

So I turned to his mom and said, "Mark likes to push me around, and he doesn't like it when I say no."

"Liar!" he fumed, hammering the table with his fist and knocking over his glass of water onto the white lace tablecloth.

"I'M NOT LYING!" I didn't mean to shout, but I was so frustrated I could barely breathe. I didn't care that everyone in the restaurant turned to look at us.

He smiled smugly, leaned back in his chair, and repeated with quiet contempt. "Liar." He folded his arms in satisfaction as if he'd proven a point.

I jumped to my feet, unsure of what I would do, but before I could think about it, Mark's parents hustled us outside, away from *Miner's Kitchen*, and back to the SUV.

We drove out of the village, and I stared at Mark the entire ten-minute trip to show him that I wasn't intimidated. He tried to ignore me, but I knew I was getting under his skin. If he was going to ruin this for me, I would ruin it for him, too.

His mom kept looking over her shoulder at us, studying us—trying to figure out what was going on, I guess, but she didn't say anything. I caught his dad looking at me briefly in the rearview mirror.

The cabin was a few minutes outside the village, a quarter of the way around the lake. I had imagined it would be an Abe Lincoln-type cabin, but it wasn't like that. It was still a simple, tiny house, but it was bigger than the one-room cabin I had imagined. There was a separate little outhouse twenty feet away—which was no more than a shack in the woods.

Mark's dad fumbled for the key and finally tripped the door lock with a loud click. The air inside was stale, as if the cabin had been abandoned for a long time, and dust particles danced in the light filtering through the windows. His mom yanked off the white sheets covering the couch and gestured for us to sit next to each other as the dust cloud settled.

His dad laid into us right away.

"We don't know what's going on with you boys, but you won't ruin the whole weekend. You're good friends, and you need to work it out."

"You—" Mark tried to protest, but his mom cut him off.

"-you two are old enough to work it out on your own. Go for a hike and talk it over. You've got half the day. Don't come back until you figure it out."

Mark didn't move, nor did I. I already knew it was a bad idea.

"NOW!" Mark's dad shouted. I jumped, and for the first time, I saw Mark flinch.

He got up, so I got up, too, and reluctantly followed him out the door.

I wasn't scared of Mark, but I knew taking a hike together was a huge mistake.

15

The Hike

Mark stomped down the dirt path and didn't look back. I wasn't surprised. He had no intention of talking to me. Honestly, I didn't feel like talking to him, either. I didn't care if we walked around the entire lake for two hours and didn't say a word. We were only doing this because his parents forced us.

The lake was in a valley far below the cabin, and the hiking path ran through the thick woods along the slope of the surrounding mountains. We passed by two other cabins in the first ten minutes, but we were mostly by ourselves. It was a steep and awkward hike. The trail wasn't very wide, and there was thick ground cover everywhere else. This would be an amazing adventure if it weren't for Mark's bad attitude.

I accepted that our friendship was doomed and that when school began again, I would be back to having precisely zero friends. Not only that but if Mark held a grudge, which was entirely possible, every day might be *Charlie Day.*

For now, though, I was trapped with someone who didn't want me around, and I would have to deal with it.

The trail switched back a few times—leading uphill ten or twenty feet, then curving downhill another ten or twenty feet, and then repeating the same pattern—I would see Mark for a while, and then he would disappear around the corner for a minute or two.

After a while, the trail returned to moving parallel to the lake, and Mark was only a dozen feet ahead of me. He was holding a thin branch he'd found somewhere, stripping the leaves from it so it was just a long, whippy stick. He swung it back and forth like a useless machete, clearing non-existent brush as he moved down the path.

I was careful to pace myself. We hadn't spoken, and I didn't want to catch up to him.

But I did anyway.

"Are you going to say anything?" I finally asked when I was just feet away.

He inspected his whip. "Nope."

He slashed at a clump of dead leaves.

"Yeah, I didn't think so."

He slashed at the leaves again, "I've got nothing to say."

"Nothing?"

"Nope."

I didn't expect anything different. The hike was useless.

"Neither do I." I couldn't wait to circle the lake. I walked on past him.

He snapped his whippy branch right across my butt. I jumped in pain.

"WHAT'S WRONG WITH YOU?" I yelled, then picked up the pace to get away from him. I felt like I might be cut under my clothes, but I didn't want to give him the satisfaction of seeing me check.

But he sprinted up to me and did it again, cracking the branch above where he hit me the first time.

I turned again and rushed toward him, snatching the stick from his hand before he could resist. In an instant, the weapon was mine.

I was filled with rage, but he just shook his head like he was disgusted, turned around, and started walking back toward the cabin.

But I wanted him to know how I felt. I wanted to whip him in the butt the same way he'd whipped me.

I wanted it to hurt.

I followed him, But just as I took my swing, he turned back toward me to tell me off.

He only managed to shout, "YOU—" before the branch slashed him across the face.

16

This Is What You Did To Your Friend

Mark's hands flew up to the side of his face as he let out a startled wail. Blood seeped between his fingers as it pulsed from the vicious cut I'd carved into his left cheek. The pain brought tears to his eyes.

I immediately dropped the stick, confused and frightened.

I wanted to say something, but I couldn't make a sound. It was like a nightmare where you try to scream, and nothing comes out.

He looked at me in disbelief, then turned and stumbled back toward the cabin.

I wanted to follow, yet I couldn't bring myself to do it.

My back was against a tree, my ragged breath struggling to find its way out of my lungs. Mark disappeared down the trail, and I felt sick to my stomach. I wanted to help him. I should have helped him. But, instead, I remained frozen where I was.

Minutes or hours might have passed as I sat there shaking uncontrollably. There were drops of his blood in the dirt, and I couldn't take my eyes away from them.

Gradually, using the tree as support, I rose to my feet again. My vision was blurred with tears, and I used my shirt to dry them before heading slowly to the cabin.

It was already late afternoon when I got there. I walked around to the gravel driveway in the front. The SUV was gone, and I thought they had left me alone and gone home.

I stared at the tire imprints, trying to figure out what to do.

The cabin door creaked open, and Mark's dad stepped out onto the little porch. He stared at me for a short time with a Mark-like death glare.

"Mark's at the hospital with his mother," he told me, his voice dripping with barely controlled rage.

"Is he okay?" I stammered, my heart beating faster.

He stared at me through narrowed eyes before responding, "Come inside." His voice was steady and cold.

Terrified, I followed him, and he barked, "Sit down."

I carefully lowered myself onto the couch. I couldn't bring myself to look up at him - I was afraid of what might happen if I did.

"I'm sorry," I muttered into my lap.

He pulled out his phone, "I want you to look at this." He pressed something and then thrust it under my nose.

On the screen was a picture of Mark's face, his skin ripped apart to reveal a raw gash running diagonally across his cheek from just under his eye to below his ear. It was smeared with blood. He swiped to the next picture, which was wider and showed his bloody shirt. Then he swiped again, this time to a close-up photo of his torn skin. Then again, to yet another angle.

My stomach turned, but I forced myself to remain still.

"Look at it!"

His voice was harsh and cutting.

"This is what you did to your friend."

I felt my heart sink in my chest as I was forced to look at the screen. I was afraid to turn away.

"How could you do this? What's wrong with you? I think you're a sick boy."

I didn't want to look at the phone anymore, but I didn't want to look at Mark's dad, either.

I barely managed to say, "I'm...sorry." I was sobbing uncontrollably.

"I really thought you were Mark's friend, but it looks like you were a mistake."

He finally put away the phone, and then I had no choice but to look at him.

"Your mother is going to drive up tomorrow to take you home."

I wondered what they told her and what she thought. The idea that Mom already knew what I'd done and would have to drive four hours to get me was terrifying.

"Can I call her?"

He hesitated, and I was worried that he wouldn't let me and I would be alone, but then he reached back into his pocket and retrieved his phone. He shoved it at me.

"Call."

I took it. Since I had become friends with Mark, I had thought about asking Mom for a phone, but I never got around to it. I wished I had.

With Mark's dad standing over me, I only spoke for a few minutes. Mom had a weird tone in her voice. I felt like she was angry at me, but I didn't want to say it aloud.

"Are you okay?"

"Yes."

"I'll be up by noon."

"Okay."

"Sooner if I can."

"Okay."

"See you then."

"Okay."

We said nothing more, but I could sense she was disappointed, and I felt more lonely than the worst *Charlie Day*. I had no idea what she would say when she saw me. I'd never made her this mad or had done anything to disappoint her like this.

But now, she knew what I was really like: I'd hurt Mark so badly that he'd gone to the hospital.

I handed back the phone, and Mark's dad went outside. Ten minutes later, the SUV came back. From inside the cabin, I could see Mark sitting in the back seat, the side of his face bandaged. He stared straight ahead and didn't look in my direction at all.

His mom exited the car, and his parents spoke briefly, then his dad walked back into the cabin.

"They're going to stay at the motel—away from you," He paused to let that sink in, "I'll be back later. If you need something to eat, it's in the pantry."

With that, he left again, and they drove off into the night, leaving me alone.

17

The Best Hamburger

For maybe half an hour, I sat on the couch, trying to understand how everything had gone so wrong. Mark had invited me. I thought he had finally trusted me. I was trying so hard to be a good friend, to be mature, and not embarrass him.

But nothing was good enough for him. Friends were supposed to accept you—not push you around or criticize you for everything. They're not supposed to think they're better than you. I made one little joke halfway up the mountain, and he hated me again.

And friends aren't supposed to whip you with a stick to get a reaction. It wasn't right, but he got a reaction—just not the one he expected. Mark probably told his parents

I went crazy, found a stick, and hit him for no reason. I guessed that's what they told my mom.

I was sure now that Mark never wanted me to be his friend. I wasn't sure why I didn't see it before, but now I did.

But I'd proven to everyone that I wasn't immature and a baby. Now, they would think of me as something worse.

I just didn't know what.

I resented having to stay in the cabin all night with Mark's dad. Mom wouldn't make it up to the mountain until noon the next day, and I didn't think I could tolerate being around his hatred for that long. He was worse than Mark.

I had to get away.

My backpack was leaning against the sofa where I'd left it when we had arrived hours earlier. I grabbed it and left the cabin.

I walked back up the short gravel driveway to the paved road that hugged the side of the mountain. I figured I could follow it back into the village, get someone to let me call Mom on their phone, and then tell her that she had to come up tonight. If I begged her and told her what was really going on, I was pretty sure she would do it.

There aren't any streetlights on mountain roads, of course, so I walked as close to the edge as possible and hoped nobody was driving crazy. It had taken us ten minutes to drive to the cabin from the village, but I had no idea how long it would take to get back there on foot. An hour?

I'd never seen so many stars in my life. I was amazed, but it made me feel as alone as I'd ever felt. I had no one in the world to share it with.

I walked down the roadway for almost half an hour before I came to the large "Welcome to Miller Lake" sign—which faced the other direction. I realized I was heading the wrong way.

I turned around and walked back, passing the cabin and heading uphill toward the village. I felt stupid.

Miner's Kitchen was even busier than at lunchtime, with packed tables inside and out. Mom had given me some pocket money for the weekend, so at least I could eat dinner. I put in my name and waited.

After fifteen minutes, a small table finally opened up all the way in the back, and I sat down.

"I'm Denise; how are you today?"

Denise, the server, was an older lady with long, steely grey hair she wore in a long braid down her back. She had a friendly smile.

"Hi, Denise."

"Are your mom and dad joining you?"

I smiled and shook my head, "Just me."

Her eyebrows rose in surprise. I could tell she thought I was younger than I was. I'd seen that look before.

"I'm thirteen," I told her.

"Ah..." She gave me an awkward smile.

"It's okay," I told her as politely as I could, "I'm used to it. At least you didn't give me the children's menu."

She held the back of her hand up to the side of her mouth like she was sharing a secret, "Then I really would have been in trouble!"

I immediately liked her and decided she was the person whose phone I would ask to borrow. I'd wait until after dinner, though.

I looked at an antique clock mounted on the wall. It was still only seven-thirty. There was still a chance my mom could make it by midnight, so I figured I could wait in the dark of the forest until then.

I gave Denise my order for a hamburger and fries, gulped down a glass of water, and then went to the restroom to get cleaned up.

I looked filthy. My hands were grubby, and so was my face—far more than I expected. My hair looked crazy, too. There were bits of leaves in it. I was embarrassed that Denise had seen me that way.

She probably thought I was insane.

I washed up and combed my hair, and by the time I returned to my table, my dinner was waiting for me. As soon as Denise saw me, she returned, still smiling.

"Is everything okay?"

For an instant, I wondered how she knew, but then I realized she was talking about the food.

I nodded, "Yes, thank you."

"Do you need anything?"

I checked. The ketchup was already on the table.

"No, I'm good."

The hamburger was the best one I'd ever tasted—maybe because I could eat it peacefully without worrying about Mark judging me.

By the time I finished my hamburger and the last of my fries, I had calmed down. I decided I was ready to make the call. As I hoped, Denise let me use her phone, though I lied and told her I'd left mine at home.

I told Mom I was calling from the cafe and got right to the point.

"I need you to come up tonight."

I was careful to keep my voice steady and serious. I didn't want to sound whiny.

I didn't want to sound like a scared little kid.

She hesitated before answering.

"I'll be up tomorrow." She was using her slow *talk-to-little-Charlie* tone, and it was unbelievably annoying. She continued, "I talked to Mark's dad—"

"NO! I'm not staying in that cabin. They don't want me there!"

I had never talked to her like this. She hesitated again.

"I can't drive up there tonight, Charlie. Now, I've talked to Mark's dad-"

"HE'S A LIAR!"

I shouldn't have shouted, but she wasn't listening to me.

"I know you're upset-"

"-forget it," I muttered sarcastically, "I'll just spend the night in the trees like a WILD ANIMAL."

I ended the call without another word, which I knew was wrong. At that moment, though, I didn't care what my mom thought.

I handed Denise back her phone and stared at my empty plate. I had no idea what I would do.

A few minutes later, she brought me a slice of apple pie.

"On the house," she told me gently. I figured she had heard me shout at Mom.

I ate the pie in tiny pieces, wanting it to last as long as possible so I could figure out where I would spend the night.

Denise came back to my table.

"The pie was great," I told her, "Thank you."

She smiled again, "You're welcome." She picked up the empty plate and then told me, "Your friends are here."

She stepped aside.

Mark and his parents were standing at my table.

18

Did You Tell Them?

I stood up right away, ready to run out. I knew instantly that my mom had called them. I looked at Mark first, and then his mom and calmly asked her, "Did he ever tell you about *Charlie Day?*"

"Let's go outside and talk," his dad said.

I sat down again and calmly sipped water like they weren't there. I hoped they would go away if I ignored them. I felt tears form, but there was no way I was going to give any of them the satisfaction.

Mark sat down opposite me.

"It's my table, so get up," I seethed, refusing to look him in the eyes. Then, I repeated what I'd said to him hours earlier: "I'm in charge."

Mark didn't move. He glanced nervously at his parents, then said, "I told them what happened."

I sipped at my water, though the glass was empty.

"I'm sorry."

I didn't believe him for a second. I finally looked up at him.

"What did you tell them?" I asked.

"What?"

"What did you tell them?"

I could tell he was nervous.

He urgently repeated his dad's question, "Can we talk outside?"

"NO!" I shouted, "WHAT DID YOU TELL THEM?"

I assumed everyone in the restaurant was looking at me, but I kept my eyes on Mark.

His mom tried calming me down, "We should take this outside. I'm sure other people don't want-"

Mark interrupted her, admitting to me, "-that I hit you first. I'm sorry."

His dad looked right at me, "Okay. Let's all go back to the cabin and talk this out."

I didn't care what his dad said. I already knew what he was like. He was as bad as his son.

Denise came by, "Can I get you anything?"

I smiled at her, "No, thank you. The check, I guess?"

"We paid already," Mark's mom said.

I folded my arms, sat back in my chair, and asked Mark, "That's all you told them?"

He looked confused.

"I don't understand."

I smirked at him with the same mean expression he gave me all the time, "Did you tell them how you treat me?"

He didn't say a word.

I screamed at him so the entire restaurant could hear, "DID YOU TELL THEM HOW YOU TREAT ME?"

He glanced anxiously at his parents, then leaned over the table, urgently whispering, "Charlie-"

"DID YOU TELL THEM HOW YOU TREAT ME? DID YOU TELL THEM?"

But then he screamed back, pointing at his bandage, "WHAT ABOUT HOW YOU TREAT ME?"

Denise rushed back to the table. I was glad she talked directly to me. I was the customer, after all.

"You should talk outside," she told me gently.

I thanked her for the pie, grabbed my backpack, and hurried out the door, ignoring Mark and his parents as they trailed me.

I didn't care what they said to me. There was no possible way I would ever return to the cabin.

As soon as we were outside the cafe, in front of a dozen people waiting for tables, I spun around and confronted Mark, "I DID NOTHING TO YOU!"

"EXCEPT MY FACE," he screamed.

"DID YOU TELL THEM HOW YOU TREAT ME?"

His mom tried again, "Let's go to the cabin."

Instead, I walked up to Mark just like he did whenever he tried to intimidate me.

But this time, he was the one who backed up. He was the one who was scared.

I closed the gap to stay close to him and kept it up until he'd backed all the to the front of the closed gift shop next door.

I thought about swinging my backpack around and smacking him with it. But, instead, I threw it on the sidewalk.

He flinched and stepped back yet again. Maybe he thought I was going to hit him.

Maybe I wanted to.

Throwing a backpack on the ground was *his* kind of thing. That was *his* signal.

Walking home from school, I always dreaded seeing Mark and his friends. I feared what was coming when he slammed his backpack to the ground and came at me. It meant something was going to happen. Getting rid of his backpack meant he wanted his hands free to hurt me—or just to frighten me.

So he knew what it meant.

I regretted ever letting him into our apartment. Why did I believe he wanted to be friends?

My hands were clenched into fists so tight that they hurt. I didn't care if he was a foot taller than me or if his parents were just feet away. I hated myself for having been so scared of him for so long.

And I hated that I kept it to myself.

Part of me wanted to hit him again, but I wasn't that kind of kid.

His dad stepped between us to keep us apart, "That's enough!"

But I wasn't done.

I looked over at Mark's mom and calmly asked her again, "Did he ever tell you about *Charlie Day?*"

19

Charlie Day

I already knew, of course, that Mark's parents would never know about *Charlie Day*. So, his mom asked him, "What is he talking about?"

Mark looked at me, answering her in just about the quietest voice possible, "I don't know." I could tell he was scared. I could tell he was hoping I wouldn't say anything.

Charlie Day was his idea, and it made everything a hundred times worse. Before *Charlie Day,* I got bullied every once in a while, but then he started the "tradition."

That's how I learned the word *sadistic*: someone who likes hurting others.

Some kids waited all week for *Charlie Day*. That made the rest of the week more bearable for me, but Fridays were the Big Game. It somehow became a competition to see how much they could do to me. Mark made it a sport to hate me.

One particular *Charlie Day* was so horrible that when I came home, filled with rage, I made a list of everything he and his gorillas did to me so I would never forget. I stopped after number thirty and threw up.

It wasn't just things like punching me or embarrassing me somehow, but little things, like breaking a pencil or drawing some gross stuff in my notebook for me to find later. People would write the same stupid things every time: "Everyone Hates You," or threaten to hurt me or tell me to kill myself. I tried not to let it get to me, but part of me was so depressed I could have cried.

But I never did.

I also knew that it wasn't every single person attacking me. Some kids never said or did anything to me. Some people even said *hi* and were kind to me in class, but it felt like Mark had created an invisible wall around me that no one wanted to cross. I didn't blame them. It actually gave me hope.

Charlie Day was so harsh and so intense that I figured some people stopped thinking of me as a person. I felt like a character in a video game that gets killed over and over again but always comes back to life.

Mark would come up to me on Friday mornings with a big grin on his face and greet me with a cheerful, "Have a happy *Charlie Day!*" like it was Christmas.

The *one* thing that kept me going was knowing it wouldn't last forever. They thought I was stupid, but at least I knew I was a good person.

And I knew he was bad.

So what was I doing *here?*

When Mark showed up at my door at the beginning of summer and said he wanted to apologize, I didn't believe him, but at the same time, it was like a dream come true. I hated him, but I wanted desperately to believe him. I wanted to believe that I had finally won out like I thought I would, and my life would change. I wanted to think that my worst enemy finally saw that I wasn't so bad. I figured if he became my friend, then anything else was possible.

So, I convinced myself to trust him, despite all the evidence.

I trust people too much.

When he said he wanted to *help* me, I believed him. I believed him when he said I was immature and acting like a baby.

I believed him when he said he wanted to be my friend. And that he could help me out.

I wanted to have a friend so badly.

When Mark wouldn't answer, his mom turned to me, "What's *Charlie Day?*"

His dad lowered his arm. He wasn't trying to keep us apart anymore.

If I wanted to, I could have grabbed Mark before they could stop me and hurt him, just like he hurt me all year. I could make all my revenge fantasies come true.

Or I could tell his parents about *Charlie Day*.

I could tell them all the things he did to me: the hitting, the slapping, the humiliation, the attacks in the school restroom, and his whole weird obsession about telling me to take a shower. I could tell them what had happened just a few hours ago when he tried to stop me from going to the bathroom.

I could ruin him.

I could get him back one way or the other, just like he got me.

But ten times worse.

His dad repeated the question this time.

"What's *Charlie Day?*"

They wanted to know, and Mark looked panicked. Usually, he shot me his death glare to intimidate me. This was different. His eyes were glassy; his skin was almost pale.

He was hoping I wouldn't tell.

But I had the power now.

This was *Charlie Day*.

20

Rage

I glanced back and forth from Mark to his mom and back to Mark again. I wanted him to know I had the power. I wanted him to be scared of *my* death glare.

I wanted him to sweat.

I looked back at his mom, ready to tell her about *Charlie Day*.

But I didn't have a chance to say anything. Suddenly, Mark collided with me from the side, and we tumbled hard down the sidewalk. By the time I realized what was going on, I was already on my back, with Mark's parents rushing toward us from twenty feet away. Mark was on top of me, his face just inches away from mine.

"WHAT ARE YOU DOING?" I screamed, struggling to push him off. I felt anger like never before and braced myself for the blows I was sure were coming.

This time, I would fight back.

But despite those few seconds of violence, Mark's rage evaporated instantly. Instead, he grabbed my collar and leaned forward, bringing his face inches from mine.

"I'm sorry-I'm sorry-I'm sorry." The words came spilling out of him in a frantic half-whisper. He was trying to get the words out before his parents caught up with us, "Don't tell them—don't tell them—don't tell them."

His eyes darted back to them and to me again. It was almost like fear. He was crying.

His dad yanked him off me, and his mom helped me to my feet. My knee was banged up and probably bloody under my pants, my arm scraped, and my head throbbed. I looked at Mark. His bandage was hanging off, and the swollen wound across his face was dripping blood again. He was panting.

With the waiting crowd outside *Miner's Kitchen* watching, Mark's parents hustled us across the street to the SUV. Mark's dad had his son's arm gripped so tightly that Mark grimaced as we stumbled across the road.

His mom sat in the back seat with me; Mark, rubbing his arm, sat in the front.

Mark tortured me the entire school year and then half the summer. I told myself I should be happy that his parents could finally see what he was really like.

But I wasn't.

We drove back to the cabin in silence. I didn't protest like I thought I would. The fight had gone out of me completely.

Somehow, it was gone from Mark, too.

I knew all of Mark's expressions. He'd trained me like a dog. I knew his *I'm going to enjoy beating you up* face, I knew his *you had better watch your back* face, and I knew, most of all, his *I'm far better than you* face.

But the expression he had when I was on the ground was entirely different.

I had no reason to care about him. He had made me feel worthless, and he didn't deserve an ounce of my compassion.

Ten minutes later, we pulled in front of the cabin, and we all climbed out of the SUV.

As his dad unlocked the cabin door, he looked at Mark with disgust, "I'm amazed at how stupid you can be sometimes."

I was wondering if I had heard that right. In my entire life, whenever my mom was angry at me, she never called me stupid. Instead, she'd say that I'd made a foolish decision or was *acting up*.

And always privately.

We walked into the cabin.

"Sit down on the couch," his father commanded.

I sat down immediately, but Mark hesitated, "Please, Dad…"

"I'M IN CHARGE! SIT DOWN!"

Mark sat down, and I felt like I'd been kicked in the stomach.

It suddenly made sense why *I'm in charge* triggered him.

Again, his mom asked him, "What was *Charlie Day?*"

Mark looked down and didn't answer. It almost looked like he wanted to cry. I had never seen him like that.

This was my perfect chance to get revenge for everything he'd done to me. An hour ago, this would have been my dream. I could tell his parents about every humiliation. Every beating. Every one of his weird "rules." I could tell them how he'd made me hate going to school. I could tell them how he's made school—and my summer—miserable. And I could show him that he couldn't do anything to stop me from telling them.

The cabin was deathly quiet. All three of them were waiting for *me* to talk.

Sitting next to him, I could almost feel Mark trembling in fear. This was the same boy who had threatened me a hundred times: *If you say anything, you'll regret it*, or *Tell anyone, I'll break your arm*.

Mark stared at his knees. I looked up at his dad, giving him back the *death glare* Mark used on me.

I felt like his dad was waiting for me to give him fuel for the fire; he wanted reasons to scream at Mark right in front of me, insult him, and bully him. He wouldn't care at all that I was sitting there. I was still angry at Mark but I knew right from wrong.

And his dad was wrong.

So I shrugged and told them all, "It was nothing."

21

Getting What I Deserve

"Are you sure?" Mark's mom asked. She was suspicious.

I shrugged again.

His mom sighed, and his dad rubbed his forehead. They didn't know what to do. They knew I was hiding something.

Too bad, I thought to myself. It's *Charlie Day*. My rules. I looked at his parents confidently.

Maybe they would ask Mark another time, but they weren't going to get it out of me.

"We're all going home tomorrow morning," his mom said after a moment, "I told your mom she doesn't need to come up."

Out of the corner of my eye, I could see that Mark was looking at me.

"Good," I told her. For the first time, I liked my voice. It felt strong.

"Are you over this?" his dad asked us warily, gesturing at nothing specific.

Mark eyed me for an instant, then looked up at his dad. "Yes, sir."

His dad looked at me for confirmation, but I said nothing.

Reluctantly, Mark's mom told us to get some sleep, and his parents retreated into the cabin's second room, closing the door behind them.

After a moment, Mark whispered, "Thank you."

I got up and brought my backpack to one of the two cots against the far wall.

"Can we forget this happened?" he pleaded. "Charlie? I could tell them we're okay, and maybe we could stay."

I pulled back the blanket, "Your dad shouldn't talk to you like that." Then, I turned to face him, "But just so you know, that's no excuse."

He looked at the floor.

"I know. I'm sorry."

I headed for the door outside to use the outhouse, pausing momentarily as I remembered something.

"Isn't that what you said to me when you first came over? That you're sorry?"

I didn't wait for an answer. Instead, I pushed the door open and left.

After the outhouse, I decided to stay outside for a while. I stood by the back of the cabin, where I could see a slice of the lake below and take in the sky above.

It felt good to breathe in the cool mountain air.

I heard Mark walk up beside me, leaves crunching beneath his feet.

"Hey, Charlie."

I ignored him and kept looking up at the stars.

"Charlie? Are we good?"

Instead of answering, I asked him a question.

"Why did you come over?"

He hesitated.

"I just wanted to see if we were good."

"No, I mean the first time. When you came and knocked on my door."

"To apologize."

"But why *then*?" Why did you wait until school ended and you already had your last *Charlie Day*?"

He didn't answer for a few seconds.

"I don't understand."

"Why *then*?"

I heard him sigh.

"Does it matter?"

"I got my head slammed into a brick wall on the last *Charlie Day*, so yeah. It matters."

He kicked at the ground but didn't say anything.

"Did you know *Charlie Day* made me want to kill myself?"

I heard something scurrying through the woods nearby and an owl hooting in the trees above us. Then, something in the distance howled.

He finally answered in a small, quiet voice.

"No."

"I didn't think so."

"I'm sorry," he said, "I just want us to be good again."

I took a deep breath and repeated myself.

"You made me want to *kill* myself, Mark."

I came so close to crying, but I kept it together. I started walking back up the trail we'd hiked earlier, wanting to get away from him before I lost it entirely.

He followed me.

"I'm sorry," he said again.

I stopped and looked at the lake in the valley below. The still water reflected the few lights on the opposite shore.

"Sorry?"

I turned to face him. I noticed he'd washed the new blood from his face but hadn't bandaged the wound again.

Our eyes locked.

"Yes."

"Friday, March Eighth."

"What?"

"At 7:56 am, I got slapped in the back of my head walking into school. I didn't know who it was."

"It wasn't me."

I could still picture my *Charlie Day* list, handwritten on one piece of notebook paper that I'd split into two columns.

"Number Two: 7:59 am, I got kicked in the butt. I didn't know who it was."

"It wasn't me."

"It was *Charlie Day,*" I reminded him, "Your thing."

I'd memorized the entire list just to cope. To build up my hatred and remind myself not to give up.

"Number Three: 8:10 am, I get jabbed in the arm with a pencil while I sit at my desk just doing my work. *That* was you."

"I'm sorry."

"Number Four: 8:56 am, another slap in the head, walking out of class. That was you, too."

"Okay, I get it." He wanted me to stop, "I'm sorry."

"Number Five: 9:10 am, I discover that someone slashed the pocket of my backpack again. It happened so many times before, so I learned not to keep anything in that pocket. I went through five backpacks last year."

"I'll pay you back," he said. His voice cracked.

"Number Six: 9:38 am, your friend David shoved me into some kid I didn't know. Then *that kid* shoved me."

"I get it," he said. "How do you remember all this?"

I spoke twice as fast.

"Number Seven: 10:10 am, I spent the nutrition period in the library because that's what Charlie had to do on *Charlie Day*. Number Eight: 10:43 am, I discover that someone wrote inside my notebook—again—that I should kill myself. Number Nine: 11:18 am, PE on *Charlie Day,* a basketball to the back of my head. You said, "Oops," like it was a big mistake. Number Ten: 11:22 am, I get another slap on the head. That was you again."

Mark held his hands up as if surrendering, "I'm not sure what you want me to do."

"That's only *ten*, and it wasn't even lunchtime yet. I counted thirty *Charlie Day* things that one day."

"Charlie, let's just tell them we worked it out. We could still have a good weekend."

"So why did you want to be my friend?" I asked again, "*Why then?*"

He stared at me for a few seconds, "I'm the one who put your head into the brick wall."

I wasn't surprised, "And then you suddenly felt sorry for me? That's a lie."

"I-I wanted to be *your* friend because..." Mark hesitated, as if it were hurting him to speak, "...because after my friends saw me do that, I had no friends."

I remembered seeing all the blood on my hands, so I couldn't feel sorry for him. I figured his friends saw it too. They figured him out a lot earlier than I did.

I used to be so desperate to make a friend that I would do anything—or say anything. Or agree to anything.

But *that* wasn't me anymore.

Despite how messed up this was—how depressing this whole summer turned out—I was looking forward to school in the fall. I felt like a different Charlie now. A better Charlie. A stronger Charlie.

Friendship with me was worth something.

Mark showed me that.

I went back to the cabin and left him standing there.

***

When we pulled up outside my apartment building hours later, Mark walked up with me while his parents waited in the car. He even grabbed my backpack and carried it to the door.

We'd barely spoken to one another coming back down from the mountains. I wouldn't talk to him, and he was afraid to speak to me.

He tried asking me one last time, "Are we good?"

I looked up at him. Maybe he meant it, but I wasn't sure how much I trusted him.

"Not yet."

He put my backpack in front of the door and smiled cautiously, "That wasn't a *no*."

"It wasn't a yes," I warned him.

I didn't return his smile. I could see that it made him feel awkward.

"I guess I'll see you later," he said and started to walk away.

"Later." I was careful not to sound too friendly.

I'm not saying I won't forgive him eventually.

But not yet.

Thank you for reading *Getting What I Deserve*.

If you or someone you know has been affected by bullying, help is available. If you can't find help close by, here are some helpful resources available online:

- **StopBullying.gov** offers general information and resources in multiple languages.

- **The Trevor Project:** TheTrevorProject.org supports LGBTQ+ youth.

- **988 Suicide and Crisis Lifeline:** Anywhere in the USA, dial 988, or chat at 988lifeline.org

A Note from the Author

Writing isn't only about expressing yourself; it's about creating something that other people enjoy, are moved by, or how they learn a new perspective.

When I was ten, I wrote a short science fiction play, and my teacher sent my friends and me out to perform for the lower grades. Complete with costumes and sound effects, we entertained half the school, classroom by classroom.

In junior high school, I created an idea for a science fiction television series. This was long before video was readily available, so it existed only on paper. I was excited when several friends joined me in this creative exercise, designing sets and costumes and writing scripts, all for the fun of doing something together. I created super-8 film movies with my friends and planned countless others that never saw the light of day. When someone in my English class found my humorous rhymes entertaining, I created one daily to make them laugh. When I wrote a short story for extra credit in English class, my teacher didn't believe I could have written it over the weekend. I had to bring in a signed note from my father proving my honesty!

I learned that writing was my superpower. Throughout school, I always knew I had *something special* that would pull me through.

I knew kids like Charlie and Mark. If I'm being totally honest, I was a bit like both of them. Growing up is complicated, and understanding your self-worth can be challenging at thirteen. You make mistakes, try to learn from them, and hopefully improve. Charlie is fictional, but I'm proud of him for learning to stand on his own two feet and not look for validation from others.

He went through a painful process and came out stronger—and you can bet that he would be the best friend you could ever have *because he knows what that means.*

I hope you've enjoyed Charlie's journey and that you find your own superpower. Please share "Getting What I Deserve" with friends and on social media, and I hope you'll **post reviews** to let others know your thoughts about the story.

Thank you for your support.

Rich Samuels, 2024

Also by Rich Samuels

Alexander Adventures: Part One
"My Life at the Bottom of the Food Chain"

Alexander Adventures: Part Two
"Own the Scrawny"

Alexander Adventures: Part Three
"My Epic Life"

"SoupChad"

***

Join us at **RichPerceptions.com**

Printed in Great Britain
by Amazon